Kiss & Tell Tail

~o~

Reverse Harem Fairy Tales

Book 1

TIMEA TOKES

ISBN: 9798675308866

DEDICATION

To all my lovely readers out there. Remember, no matter what your dreams are (naughty or not), you have everything you need to make them come true.

If you love my writing style, please check out my other titles on Amazon, and follow me on my blog & website for a FREE pdf copy of Squirm Under My Watch, FREE Audiobooks, and other goodies, to say a personal thank you to you all.

I am also hosting a monthly signed paperback giveaway, with at least 2 winners each month. So, please stay tuned, and share the love that's deep inside all of you.

Thank you!

www.timeatokes.com

ACKNOWLEDGMENTS

All characters and events in these stories are purely fictional, therefore any resemblance to real people (living or dead) or events is a coincidence.

All characters would be at least 18 years of age, too, should they be real.

Caution: Contains descriptive sex scenes and adult contents.

Intended for a mature audience of at least 18+ (or more, depending on your country of residence and the local law).

Chapter 1

~o~

W hat's your name, beautiful?"

His question makes me want to retch. Why? Well, firstly, because I have no idea who he is. And secondly, because I have no idea who *I* am. Therefore, I can't answer his question. Oh, and thirdly, I have no idea whether I'm beautiful or not. Just for the record.

Bile rises up in my throat, and I'm faced with the simple question: do I give in and ruin my chances of knowing more about this handsome stranger, or do I swallow? His dark eyebrow raises, increasing my pulse. Why am I so attracted to him? Is he even my type? And why the hell can't I remember anything except...

Swallow it is.

"I um..."

Smooth.

I clear my throat then try again.

"I'm Eve."

Simple, elegant, easy to remember. I flinch at the irony, but he simply looks up at the powder-blue sky, chewing on the name. I'm not sure I want to deceive him like this, but the other alternative is far less tempting. Whoever he is, I don't think he would appreciate a crazy girl, stranded on the beach, wrapped in nothing but a bedsheet, who can't even remember her name.

"Eve. Just as gorgeous as you are."

I'm tempted to roll my eyes at him, and it takes all I have not to do just that. Well, I guess it's a good sign. Even though I don't remember a thing, I still recall this being the cheesiest pick-up line ever. Okay, there *is* something nagging at my subconscious, so I'm not entirely clueless. I might even be crazy after all. What other explanation could there be?

I woke up on this beach a few hours ago, mind completely blank. Yep, like a white sheet of paper when a writer sits down to create a story. I don't even know how I came up with that comparison. It seems like I still have my sense of humour – or I might have developed it after whatever happened that took my memories away. Well, *I* find myself funny anyway.

It was still dawn when I was finally able to look at my surroundings. The agonising pain in my head and my lower torso was almost unbearable, so I took a while sitting up. And when I did, I screamed. Partly because of the jolt of pain shooting down to my bum, and partly because I was stark naked.

"Earth calling Eve. Anyone home?"

Okay, he is beginning to annoy me now. A girl can't even have a moment to themselves, trying to figure it all out? Apparently not. Oh well, not that I made much progress anyway. With a sigh I roll my eyes. God, that felt good.

"I'm sorry, it's just... So many things happened to me lately, I'm still trying to wrap my head around it all."

I hope it's not a lie. It's generic enough, right? Lots of things happen to people all the time, I guess. But what do I know? He seems to be convinced though as he nods. I notice how he is trying to keep his eyes away from my half-exposed curves. My eyes aren't even half as co-operative. I gulp.

"I understand. Trust me, I do."

His crystal eyes take on a dreamy hue, and I want to know his story so badly right now, it hurts. God, I want to know it even more than I want to know mine. And trust me, that was all I could think about since I woke up. He clears his throat and the vibration sends shivers down my spine. I supress a groan when the pain shoots down to my bum once more. This isn't good. I'm no expert, but looking at the facts, something must be wrong with me.

"Please don't take this the wrong way, but do you have somewhere to stay?"

I don't know, do I?

I close my eyes, forcing the memories to surface. I wait a few moments, but nothing. Well, except for the now constant voice telling me I have to kiss this guy before it's too late. I shake my head in an attempt to get rid of the voice, but he must take it as a negative answer, because he clears his throat again. Déjà vu. Electric shock down my spine, pain in my butt.

Literally.

"Again, I hope you don't mind me saying this, but I do happen to have an empty room at my place. Just till you can get back on your feet."

A laugh escapes me. Yeah, right, he didn't mean that literally. How could he know that right now I have difficulty standing? Not to mention the voice in my head, or the memory loss. Staying at his place? Bad idea. No, scrap that. Worst idea ever. But then again, who knows what was my worst idea ever?

Exactly.

"If I say yes, do you promise not to kill me?"

I bite my lip, afraid to ask him the other version. You know, when the innocent girl would ask the handsome stranger to be a gentleman. There are only two problems with that one. I am scared of his answer, and I don't think I want him to be a gentleman, which scares me even more. Bad idea number two. But what option do I have, really? His warm laughter brings me back to reality. My new reality, I guess. A rush of adrenaline, followed by excruciating pain.

Sweet.

"I don't make promises I can't keep."

He winks at me, and if it wasn't for the pain, I would laugh again. I force a faint smile though, and concern clouds his features for a moment.

"Are you hurt?"

Am I?

I nod weakly, rubbing my arms. I feel cold, hungry, and lost. How do I even begin explaining this? He holds out a hand, and I take it after a moment's hesitation. Gently, but surely, he hauls me to my feet, but as I stumble and another jolt of pain rushes through my entire body when my feet hit the ground, he furrows his brows.

"Maybe I should take you to a doctor first..."

I don't know why, but alarm bells ring loud and clear in my head at the mention of a doctor. Not sure why I'm scared so much, but right now my gut feeling is all I have, so I will roll with it.

"No, please."

I grab his arm, partly for support, and partly because it feels good. It feels safe. *He* feels safe.

"I mean, I'm okay, really. All I need is some food, clothes, and rest. Lots of the latter."

I manage a smile again, and this time his searching eyes land on my lips. They tremble in response, and I feel a strange tingling sensation between my thighs. It takes me by surprise, because I don't recall ever feeling anything like this. Okay, that might not mean much, considering, but still, it's weird. I decide to brush it off for now.

"Well, if you are sure?"

I nod again, feeling a bit more certain myself.

"Lead the way."

He looks at me for a second, then says in his deep, oceanic voice:

"I have a better idea."

And with that, he picks me up in his arms, carrying me away from the beach. I want to protest, but this feels really good. I think I let out a satisfied moan, because he chuckles, his chest rumbling against my cheek. I put my arms around his neck tightly, afraid to let go.

You must make him kiss you before it's too late.

The voice inside my head is the last thing I notice before my eyes stoop and a blissful darkness envelopes me...

~o~

Chapter 2

~o~

I have the weirdest dream ever. I'm swimming in the deepest parts of the ocean, watching as delicate rays of the afternoon sun caress the waves. The water in return embraces the light, making it its own, millions of tiny fractures floating around me. I'm part of the water, I'm one with the ocean and its creatures. I can hear the whales sing, and I sing with them, heart content and full of joy. The sound reverberates through the waves, making me tingle all over.

And then I notice him swimming towards me. He is the most gorgeous creature I've ever seen. Eyes green and fluorescent, reflecting the light the same way the waves do. Hair as red as the flames of fire, with a hint of ginger and blond here and there. The contrast mesmerises me, and I know I'm staring, but I can't help it. The rest of his body doesn't even register at first, but when it does, I let out a small whimper.

Where his legs should be, he is sporting a tail as fluorescent and green as his eyes. It's covered by scales, just like a fish's, although they are much bigger and more beautiful. I find myself reaching out and caressing one after another. They feel silky under my touch, and the tingling sensation returns between my thighs.

I glance down, only to realise that I have a tail to match his, in a gorgeous array of silver and myriads of shades of green. Moss, emerald, baby green. His deep voice makes me lose count of all the hues.

"I'm Sebastian. It's a pleasure to meet you, Ariel."

I blink up at him, and he bows down, slowly disappearing from view. And so does the ocean, now covered by a shadow. I hear an evil laughter, then the voice from my nightmares sends shivers down my spine, and not the good kind:

"You should have stayed with him, little mermaid. But because you didn't, you will soon be mine."

A sudden pain forces me to look down again, and murky water swirls around my bottom half. The pain grows unbearable, forcing me to close my eyes. When I open them again, I'm no longer in the ocean's warm embrace. I'm lying on a crisp white sheet, covered by thick blankets. I examine the pink blossoms that are printed on them for a few moments, before kicking them off with way too much force.

My tail is gone, and in its place are two human legs. Was I dreaming a moment ago, or is this a dream? I could breathe easily under the water, and now I don't seem to have an issue, either. Of course, this makes sense if one of these realities is a dream. But which one? Having no memories of my past and no prospects for my future, which version do I trust? In my mind, everything seems like it's full of danger.

Going back under sounds rather tempting though, and Sebastian's smooth voice still rings in my ears, but the faint sounds of laughter reach my subconscious, not letting me fall back into the idea of going back to sleep (if that's what I was doing in the first place). I listen for a while, and although the sound is unfamiliar, a pang of longing settles in my heart.

The questions I had before have only multiplied, and I'm not sure where all this is going to take me. I'm only certain of two things: I won't rest until I find out what's going on. And the second, *well...*

My stomach churns, and that settles that. I'm hungry. Placing one foot onto the floor, followed by the other, then try to get up. The ball of my foot hurts, and my feet land in an unnatural angle, so I need to hold onto the bedframe. I grasp the thick wood, glancing down at my toes, like I've never seen them before.

Well, have I?

I let out a sigh, bracing myself for another fall, but I only wobble a little, and the pain shooting down to my butt is quite bearable this time, so I decide it will have to do for now. I straighten my spine, preparing myself for an encounter I'm not ready for. Just when I'm about to take my first step, the voice inside my head takes me completely off guard.

Hurry, you only have three days to kiss him with true love's first kiss.

I stumble to the floor, panting heavily, tears streaming down my face. Yeah, right, this is so wrong on so many levels. I don't think I believe in true love, for one. And besides, how on Earth do I achieve that in such a short period of time, when I don't even remember why I have to do it in the first place? Although, judging by the circumstances, I'm quite confident that I had a very good reason. I just have to find a way to remember it before it's too late.

~o~

Chapter 3

~o~

As I stumble towards the door, my reflection catches my eye, making me blink and think twice of my next move. A stranger is looking back at me, but one I don't mind. I know it sounds funny, but if I didn't know it was me in there, I wouldn't believe it. I mean, what do I have to go on?

Okay, so now I know what Eric meant. Although I don't trust any of my memories or dreams, surely, I can trust the mirror and the reflection staring back at me. I might still be unsure what's classed as beautiful, and I know it's always a question of perspective, but my own perspective is telling me right now that I belong to that category.

It might be that I just need to feel better about something, I don't know. But, right now, my reflection is the only thing I wouldn't change. Funny how losing your memory puts everything in said perspective. Would I still think I looked nice, should I get my memories back? Who's to say I wasn't one of those ungrateful women who always wanted more? A flatter stomach, a different shade of hair, bluer eyes, bigger boobs. The list goes on, I would imagine.

But no. My eyes are as big as saucers, shining bright in the candlelight. They are gorgeous, I must say, surrounded by thick, black eyelashes and a nicely shaped, also black brow. And their colour is… Well, it's a mixture of blue and green, myriads of shades of both, and a circle of amber around my pupil. Fascinating. Do many people have eyes like these where I come from?

Where do I come from?

The dream from moments ago comes to mind, and a ridiculous idea with it. Of course, when you have no idea who or even what you are, you begin to doubt that you are human to begin with. Those scales and the water, that guy... Merman, was it? Right, what's next, bloody unicorns? I turn out to be a phoenix, rising from its ashes, starting a new life as a human?

True, my hair would support that theory for sure. A bit similarly to the merman in my dreams, my hair is a fiery red. The only difference is that mine is *really* red, as in crimson. Is that normal? I have no idea. But then again, I could have dyed it, surely. Hmm, it seems like I wasn't that satisfied with myself after all.

Hurry, you will have time to admire yourself later. Now, we are running out of time.

I turn around quickly, hoping that someone is in the room with me. Sadly, deep down I know that the voice is in my head. If the gods took away everything from me, why leave the voice? Or did I acquire it *after*? To keep me sane?

Oh, the irony.

And yet, I feel what it's talking about. The nagging pit in my stomach grows more painful the more time passes. I know I ought to do something, but what that is, I'm not certain.

You are going to figure it out. That's why I...

Great, now the voice is not only talking in riddles, but doesn't finish its sentences, either. Yep, I am going mad. Well, I can only hope it happens faster than whatever is threatening to take me. Which poses a really important question: am I a prisoner?

Grabbing the bathrobe that's hanging off the back of a chair by my bed, I wobble out the door and into the foyer. Yep, my legs still don't work like they used to. Or at least I hope they used to work. I shake my head again, trying to get rid of these ridiculous notions. Starting to doubt every single thing about my previous (and current) existence won't do me any good. Not at all.

You can do this. One step at a time. I have faith in you, Ariel.

And there it is again. Ariel. Is that my name? Sounds unlikely. I guess I just conjured it up in my subconscious, just the way I did with this mystery guy, this Sebastian. Well, he isn't exactly a guy per se, but still.

I sigh, reluctantly obliging. Left foot, right foot, then another left. It's all about small triumphs, right? As I slowly walk down the stairs, my eyes wonder aimlessly, and so does my heart and my thoughts go with it. And, as much as I don't want to, I feel lost, scared and a tiny bit fascinated by it all. The gorgeous paintings on the wall, the mahogany railing, the velvety carpet under my bare feet... It's all new, yet familiar somehow.

What am I supposed to do now? Is anyone coming to get me? Unlikely. But surely, I have someone looking for me? The remnants of my dream swim to the surface yet again, and this time I let them linger for a moment.

For someone who doesn't recall a thing, I sure as hell have weird-ass dreams. And that longing I feel? It's so weird, because I could swear that in my dream, I felt at home in the ocean's warm embrace. I longed for Sebastian's voice to sooth me, like a mother's voice comforts a sick child. No, not that way. You don't want a mother to comfort you in the way I wanted Sebastian to comfort me. And yet, upon waking and hearing Eric laughing in the background, I felt home, too. No, *he* felt like home.

Nonsense. This is real, that was just a dream. Or am I really losing my mind now, and the memory loss was just the first sign? Well, I guess that after the kind of day I had, even that wouldn't surprise me. Yep, I must have hit my head pretty hard.

'Eve?'

Eric's voice makes me look up and stumble at the same time. And then I fall. I close my eyes, as if that could help. Still, the darkness is so welcome that I decide to stay a while. It's reassuring, safe. Just like the ocean...

~o~

Chapter 4

~o~

'm swimming again. My feet are replaced by a tail, as gorgeous as Sebastian's. I watch, mesmerised, as the rays of the setting sun from above cast their shadows on the scales, giving them hundreds of ethereal hues. It tickles a bit, and the tingling sensation travels through my entire body.

Sebastian cocks his head to the side, shaking it slowly. The corner of his upper lip wobbles, and I know he is trying desperately not to laugh at me. He has always thought me to be childish, but then, he was always the one to join me on my secret adventures.

Oh, how many secrets the two of us shared.

I blush, the memory still as vivid as if it happened yesterday, and he raises an eyebrow. I beckon him closer, with a seductive vibration leaving my throat. It doesn't take him long to swim my way, allowing me to watch as this magnificent creature so desperately wants to be mine yet again. Maybe later. Now I have other plans.

The shock is palpable on his handsome face when he leans in to kiss my neck, and I lean back, splashing him with water. Okay, maybe a bit of mud, too. He hoovers there for a few seconds, and I wait breathlessly for his next move. I don't have to wait long, as he lounges at me, making me squeak. But to be fair, the vibration the sound sends through the ocean turns me on. And I know it has the same effect on him. We have played this game many times before.

Now, with my hands pinned above my head, and Sebastian's weight on top of me, I don't want anything more. He is mine, and I am his. Always. We are free, we are in love, and we are happy. And nobody can take that away from us. Not even...

A dark shadow clouds my vision for a moment, bringing stormy rays into Sebastian's gaze, but as soon as it arrives, it vanishes. It must have been a ray. Nothing to worry about. Unless...

No, I mustn't think about that now. Sebastian kisses me passionately, and I don't resist anymore. Slowly, the memory of the potential threat fades into nothingness, and all there is, once more, is the two of us, making love on the seabed. My tail slowly begins to vibrate, giving way to two long and beautiful legs. Sebastian always tells me that my human form is gorgeous, with all the right curves.

'You are the most beautiful creature I ever met.'

He whispers, stealing a kiss, my hands still pinned above my head. I can't help but feel naked every time my tail does that, but I also know it's essential for our lovemaking and his tail will follow suit. The magic deep within us is so great it allows us to channel the energies of all the elements. We learnt the human ways, and because we liked it so much, we decided to go with it.

'You are the most handsome creature I've ever met, too.'

I say, knowing too well that it isn't enough to describe how I feel about Sebastian. Mermaids aren't meant to be settled down with only one partner, but what we have is so special that I don't want to ruin it. I know he would understand, and that I could tell him all my secrets, but I don't want to. I want to keep us this way for as long as I can.

Sebastian shifts his hips, grinding them against me, and he soon finds a seaweed to tie my hands with. He does the same with my legs, connecting them at the ankles. He flips me onto my stomach, the water carrying my weight and I raise an eyebrow at him over my shoulder, watching as his impressive cock springs to life. His tail has vanished as well, which means he is ready.

I let out a sigh, remembering the times when merfolk only had sex to reproduce. Things are different now. Just like humans, we change as the times and customs change, too. As I said, what works for them in their world, works for us down here. If anything, we have found different ways to carry out their kinky ways.

'Well, well, I'm in trouble again.'

I say cheekily, wiggling my butt at him. He raises an eyebrow, smirking. His hand is on my ass in a second, and his eyes follow suit soon enough.

'I miss your ass when it isn't here.'

He muses, running a finger down my crack, making me shiver. My throat vibrates and I watch a colourful ray of fish swim by, looking at us. Funny how humans have an issue having sex in the open, saying that it's all wrong. I never felt so alive. Sex is a natural act based on our most primal instinct. And, to be fair, doing it wherever and whenever, without any inhibitions is where we differ from humans. We don't shy away from our desires, pretending to be something we are not.

One could say that we pretend to be human for the duration of the act, but that's not true, either. My mother used to tell me thousands of stories of magical mermaids that could transform at will and go onshore for however long they preferred. Occasionally they even chose a mate from there, or several mates. And once they taught them how to use the magic that's in every living creature, they joined her in the ocean, visiting earth every now and then.

'You are so beautiful.'

Sebastian's voice brings me back to the present and I roll my eyes at him.

'You said that before, my love. So, are you going to spank that ass you admire so much or not?'

I don't have to tell him twice. We both learnt a lot of dirty talk from humans, and it does feel exhilarating. His hand comes down onto my sensitive skin, and he produces that delicious vibration in his throat, matching mine. The combined mixture makes me wet instantly. He positions me so that my ass is up in the air, before opening my cheeks.

I close my eyes as the cool ocean air caresses my body, and wait for the delicious moment when our bodies become one. But Sebastian isn't rushing. He produces another seaweed, now tickling my back with it, moving all the way down to my crack. I let out a soft moan and he slides the seaweed along my pussy lips.

He moves it to my clit, and the tingling sensation almost makes me cum, especially that I can't move. I could of course get out of the situation by switching my legs for my beloved tail, but what would be the fun in that? Then we wouldn't have a chance to live out our craziest fantasies. And I won't have any of that.

'I'm ready whenever you are.'

I hiss, but Sebastian places a soft kiss on my back, starting his sweet torture with the seaweed once again, moving up and down my spine.

'Not so fast, princess. You need to learn discipline...'

He trails off, kissing my lower back.

'Patience...'

Another kiss just above my bum and a lick of the seaweed on my clit.

'Perseverance...'

I gulp when he tickles my other hole with the seaweed, inserting it slightly. I push my ass higher up, so he has better access. I gain a smack from him and I glance back over my shoulder again. The familiar heat is burning in his gorgeous eyes, and I send him a telepathic message, tired of words:

Sebastian, I can't take this anymore. You need to give me what I want.

He smirks at me, cocking his head to the side. Opening my ass cheeks wide, he lowers himself down, seaweed in hand. I close my eyes, realising that he isn't going to give in this time. He is the one who wants to dominate, having learnt that from the human males. We watched them many times, and I must admit, out of all their habits, this turned me on the most.

Being dominated by your chosen partner is empowering, even if it doesn't seem that way. And not to mention that the orgasms I have shared with Sebastian over the past millennia have been epic. And it's only getting better with all the kinky stuff the humans come up with. All we need to do is watch and learn and adapt.

'Um, yes, just like that...'

I moan as Sebastian's tongue darts into my folds, exploring them the same way we always explore the ocean together. His tongue promises to be there all the time, for as long as I want it to be.

'You taste so sweet. Even sweeter than last time.'

I blush, remembering the last time Sebastian licked me out this way. He doesn't know what brought my arousal on back then, but still, he was ready to please me every way he could. A sigh escapes me when he smacks my left cheek, while teasing my asshole with the seaweed and sucking on my clit at the same time.

'I'm almost there.'

I whisper, and he stops. I glance back over my shoulder again, eyes hooded with desire, and he smirks at me once more.

'I am not giving you permission to cum yet. You need to earn that bit.'

And with that, he pushes the seaweed deeper, and my hole opens up for him. He also decides to use this moment to start fingering my pussy, abandoning his mission to make me cum by licking me out. I wiggle as much as I can, but he still has my ankles tied together. If he doesn't let me cum yet, I decide to enjoy the moment, trying to distract myself.

It isn't easy though, because so many years of learning the best ways to please each other had their effect: Sebastian is a master of my body, mermaid and human alike. He can set it on fire, or cool it down with a single touch, depending on what he wants. And the thought that he has so much power over me is intoxicating and arousing as hell.

'How do I earn something like that? You will keep telling me I need to do more.'

I whimper, watching a crab crawl by. I contemplate doing the same, but it would be no use. And I don't really want to escape this sweet torture anyway. Sebastian rewards me by inserting a second finger into my aching pussy.

'By being a good girl and not trying to escape.'

I moan loudly when he finds my G-spot (which is funny, because we would normally call it the O-spot, but we have adapted in this way as well), and my inner muscles clench. I can't help it and Sebastian knows that. Even after fucking me a thousand times, and even after me trying to control myself around him for the past millennia, I am still unable to. I'm completely lost when I'm with him, but in a good way.

'Was I good enough there?'

I ask, wiggling my butt once again. He laughs, but when I glance back, he is sporting his tail again. A frown appears on my face as I prop myself up on my elbows, hopping in the mud. I must look funny, because his laughter gets louder, sending vibrations through the ocean and my body.

'Wasn't I?'

I ask, motioning towards his tail (and rather his lack of erection), but he shakes his head, his laughter easing into a gentle smile.

'You were. And it isn't like I'm not in the mood, but I wanted to please you this time and admire your beauty.'

A strange cloud passes over his face, one that I haven't seen during our thousand years together, but it's gone as soon as it arrived. I'm a bit annoyed, because I expected sex. Lots of it. But I guess it's fine. It has to be.

'Fine. You going to untie me then?'

Sebastian's grin turns cheeky and he winks at me, spanking my butt once more before snapping the seaweed holding my ankles together.

'What about my hands?'

I ask, but he shakes his head, planting a swift kiss on my lips.

'You need to earn that, too.'

He snuggles in next to me, and we talk about the human ways we want to learn next. I tell him that I always wanted to taste Indian food, because humans seem to be so keen on it, but Sebastian reminds me of the chef we watched barf his guts out after eating said food, so I agree that I should put that to the end of my bucket list.

We laugh and sing, riding the waves afterwards, and I listen to (or rather feel) the way they vibrate with the sound, enveloping me. Welcoming me. I'm home. And he is mine. He leans in for a swift kiss, one that almost doesn't register in my brain, but one that's enough to make my heart flutter.

I am home. He is my home.

But my happiness doesn't last long, as the terrifying shadow reappears, threatening to destroy everything I hold dear. Her evil laughter travels through the waves, setting my skin on fire and sinking my heart. No, she can't take this away from me. I won't let her. Even if she knows my deepest secrets, and even if she wouldn't stop at anything to use them against me. Sebastian can never find out the truth...

He looks at me, concern in his gorgeous green eyes. Of course, he can't see the sea-witch, nobody can. Nobody, except for those unlucky few she deems worthy. Or rather, who she wants as her next prey. Yay, I guess I should be thrilled I made the list. The shadow disappears again, and only her raspy voice that's still ringing in my ear is a reminder that she was ever here. God, how long was she watching us for?

Did she...

'Are you okay, my love?'

Sebastian caresses my flushed cheeks, and I nod meekly. There's no need to worry him, not until Ursula comes forward and tells me what she wants with me. I can deal with her teasing, with her silent threats. I know she has the power to kill me with the flick of her fingers if she so wishes, and yet I'm still here, still alive. Not to mention that I'm still enjoying Sebastian's company, which wouldn't be the case, surely, if the sea-witch wanted to kill me.

'I'm fine, I just...'

His concern intensifies, and my heartbeat accelerates in turn. Not the way I wanted this to go. I let out a sigh, shaking my head. A strand of fiery hair falls into my eyes, and I try to brush it away, but he is quicker, grabbing my hand and placing a tentative kiss onto my fingertips. The brush of his lips is so gentle, so reassuring. How could I break his heart now? How could I tell him that the future we have both planned for years might not ever happen? One way or another, Ursula always gets what she wants. And, by the looks of it, she wants me.

'I meant that I'm fine, I just wish we could do that again.'

The concern is replaced by confusion for a moment, but then I note the realization in his burning gaze. The last rays of the sun slowly fade into oblivion, and his eyes take on an unlikely shade of emerald green, almost fluorescent, thanks to the flora around us. If I didn't love him before, I would certainly fall for him. Now I do it all over again anyway.

'Fine. I think you have earned it by now.'

And with that, he steals a lingering kiss and I'm back in heaven, the sea-witch completely forgotten. Little do I know that soon she won't be the only part of my present that I'm going to forget...

A tempting taste of other, bite-size erotica, from the naughty pen of Timea Tokes:

~o~

A SPECIAL CUP OF COFFEE
(SAMPLE)

Don't worry, this is a first for me, too..."
Ah, is that supposed to comfort me?
Very promising.

I try to pull on the restraints, but he has tied me up tightly. My heart is pounding, and I can't see a thing because of the blindfold. All I can do is wait helplessly until he figures out his next move, wondering how could I have gotten myself into this mess.

A mere hour ago I was sitting at the bar, minding my own business, drinking heavily, as if there was no tomorrow. Right up to the moment when the bartender offered to make me a special cup of coffee. Which I'm still waiting for, by the way.

Just saying.

Okay, I wasn't that naïve to think that we would actually be drinking coffee, cuddling on his couch, no. And as I said, I didn't want that anyway. I wanted hot, steamy, and kinky sex. And although he hasn't touched me yet, not in that way anyway, this whole situation is kinky alright.

"Just try to relax and clear your mind..."

He is really getting into this. Does he have a guidebook that he is citing from? I must admit that hearing his voice alone makes me shiver all over. It is sexy as hell, and I can already feel the previous dampness of my thong worsening by the minute. I wonder how long is he going to keep me suspended like this? It's funny how you lose all of your senses when you can't see.

No kidding!

Although I can hear his voice, but only when he allows me to, and I still can't tell where it's coming from. For all I know he could be standing in the doorway, ready to lock me in, leaving me to suffer for God knows how long. I sure as hell hope he isn't planning to make that special cup of coffee *right now.*

But judging by what he just said, I guess I need to do the opposite. In fact, my mind is the only thing that's working perfectly well right now. And my survival instincts, of course. I begin to regret that I didn't listen to my friends. I should have waited for this kind of kink until I knew the guy, let alone trusted him.

Oh my God, I don't even know his name!

"You might feel a little bit cold. Try not to wiggle too much, okay?"

Okay, I was wrong. All my nerves are on edge, and I want to scream from the ice-cold sensation that's burning my left nipple right now.

Little bit cold?

Whatever he put on me makes me want to swear and scream, except I can't. All I can give out is a tiny whimper through my gritted teeth. I want to tell him to stop, to let me go, feeling embarrassed and exposed all of a sudden.

But as quickly as the thought forms in the back of my mind, it evaporates just as quickly when he takes my erect nipple into his mouth. His hot, wet tongue is a relief from the ice-cold sensation, and yet it feels a tad bit more painful, maybe because I am more sensitive than I ever was. He bites down gently, and I can feel the coldness on my right nipple, while he is stroking my left one with his tongue.

I gasp, getting lost in the mixed sensations of hot and cold, pain and pleasure. But it doesn't last long, and as much as I wanted him to stop at first, now I wish that he would continue the sweet torture. An involuntary moan leaves my lips, and he lets out a small chuckle.

"Don't worry, I have only just started."

His words send a jolt of electricity right down to my lady parts, and I'm sure I blush a little, too. I think about my black strapless dress, the black lace push-up bra and the black high heels scattered around the room. I'm not even sure he is wearing anything right now, as after a few passionate kisses, he moved straight onto the subject. He promised it to be fun, erotic and orgasmic.

The last part convinced me, and I'm more and more sure that he is a man who keeps his promises...

A tempting taste of the popular Paranormal Romance (slash Romantic Suspense) saga, 'Her First and Last Secret Admirer' by Timea Tokes:

HER FIRST SECRET (BOOK 1)

(SAMPLE)

They meet by accident. She dreams about him, afraid to face reality. She keeps it as a secret. Then they meet again and her world turns upside down as he makes her question all the things she once believed in. But is this the first time they go through this? Or were they more than just dreams?

"This is a story about finding love in the most unlikely of places, realizing you lose your chance to be with that person, and then letting fate take its cause until you meet again. There's also other forces at work; a mystical stranger starts sending Lia online messages and providing inspiration for her to figure her life out. As the past and present clash, a new kind of future for Lia could emerge. While it's romantic fiction and bares all of its hallmarks, I ultimately want all women to see a part of themselves in Lia. We all dream of a knight galloping in on a white horse, and my book will compel readers to weight up how much of life is fate, and how much of our destiny we create for ourselves."

There are some things you just can't tell anyone. Sometimes you don't even admit those things to yourself. You are too scared. You are confused, you don't want to accept what your heart already knows. Some people call it intuition, some deja vu, others say it is only coincidence. It might only be our mind playing tricks with us. Whatever it is, you push it to the back of your mind, as if you let it manifest, everyone (including yourself) will think you are crazy. And like this you feel safe and secure. You relax, as you managed to convince yourself that nothing is happening, you just imagined it. Until it happens all over again. And again...

You can fool yourself once, maybe even twice, but if there is a message out there for you, these signs won't stop until you listen. And you have to listen very carefully. And when you do, you will get more confused. At first you won't understand. It will take a lot of time and concentration. Will you ever figure it out completely? Will you ever be able to fill that emptiness within your soul? You know something is missing, something is not quite right. You are looking at a big puzzle, and you can't see the whole picture yet. All you have are small pieces. Pieces you have to put together in order to understand. In order to fill that hole. In order for these coincidences, deja vus to make sense. And you don't even have a guide.

Some pieces you will put in the wrong place. Several times. Until you find where they belong. And then you start over with the next one. And the one after that. Until you get halfway through. And then another piece shows up, which fits in completely – in the middle of the picture, where you already placed a different piece. And adding the new one to it, the picture changes dramatically. You start questioning yourself. You discover that you can put the pieces together in lots of different ways, and get different pictures. This time you work faster. Maybe you can even finish it.

This is the point when you get excited, and look forward to the result. You are proud of yourself. You might even be able to put two-three different pictures together. But until then you only have pieces. Until then you have to believe that you will have the whole puzzle at some point. You need to have faith. Faith to carry on solving the biggest riddle of your life. I think I made it pretty obvious what (or who) is the center piece in my puzzle. At first I did the obvious: ignored it. I thought he can't be. Cause if he was, I wouldn't be able to fill that hole. He was gone and wasn't coming back.

Or so I thought. From time to time I thought I saw his smile in crowds. Of course by the time I looked back, he was gone. I was pretty sure it was my imagination. I could live with that. At least I had the gift of "seeing" Him with my mind's eyes. Over and over again. Until it got too much. I couldn't take it anymore. Every time I "saw" Him, my heart broke a little. It wasn't enough anymore. I wanted it all...

~o~

HER SECRET ADMIRER (BOOK 2)

(SAMPLE)

He knows everything about her. She doesn't know anything about him. Or does she? Is he a stalker? Or a secret admirer? A ghost maybe? The man of her dreams? Or her worst enemy? Can she survive reality? And what about her dreams?

I hear the howling again, so I run faster. I can only hope that I will escape. I think I never ran so fast in my entire life. Well, I never had to run for my life either. In my mind I already pictured the end: the beast catching up with me and stealing my last breath while its claws dig deep into my skin. I want to scream, but then he would know where I am. I managed to hide till now, why would I give up? I am scared, but – strangely – the closeness of death fills me with another, unfamiliar feeling. It is so unnerving, and yet it keeps me going somehow.

I don't remember if I ever felt so much fear, and yet excitement at the same time. Yes, I think that's it. I am thrilled, maybe because so much is at stake. Or maybe because this whole thing could end right here and right now. No more running, no more hiding. Living in fear is worse than death itself. Never knowing who comes after you next, what sick joke he is playing with you this time. I escaped so many of his minions. I think he underestimated me. I don't blame him. I underestimated myself, too. I didn't know what I was capable of in order to survive.

Now I know. And I am not proud of it. But still, at least I am alive. I could blame myself for the things I've done to come this far. Yes, I could, easily. And I did, for a long time. But with time I had to realize that I didn't have a choice. Of course, if He was here with me, everything would be different. We would go through this together, escape the marquee's evil plan. It would be easy. But this is not how it happened. God, I don't even know if Lorian is still alive or not.

I haven't seen him since the fire. Everything happened so quickly, and they came after me. I can still feel the heat, their eyes on me, when they broke into the room and tried to kill me. I could hardly breath from the smoke, or see from my tears. I didn't have anything to fight them with, and that was what scared me most. I was vulnerable. I didn't understand that time. I didn't know why were they after me. Now I know...

HIS SECRET LOVE (BOOK 3)

(SAMPLE)

He sends her messages, pretending to be a friend. But can he ever be more? Or will the truth ruin everything? Living a life of misery, only dreams of the past can help him reclaim his lost future. Which path will he chose? Join him on the journey towards his destiny, as he has his own story to tell...

I open my eyes, but instead of the empty cell walls I can see her smile. Is this an illusion? Or am I dead and this is what heaven feels like? I cannot feel any pain anymore, so it must be the latter. I close my eyes again, enjoying the blissful feeling her soft hands are giving me, caressing my face ever so gently. I want to moan, cry, laugh and scream at the same time, but all I can manage is a weak cough. And then all the pain comes back. Not that I care.

Not this time. When I realize what's happening I want to ask her so many questions, but she simply nods, a small smile appearing on her lips. Her gaze burns my skin, moving up and down, as if trying to take every detail in before I disappear. Then her eyes rest on my bruised wrists and I can hear her gasp – not from pleasure this time. I wish she didn't have to see me like this. Probably this is one of Alex's new tricks. I couldn't care less. Now that I know that she is safe. And she doesn't seem to be hurt either.

Unless...

No, I can't think of that right now. If he did something to her, he is a dead man. I will make sure of that. But for now, I have to tell her to run. I try to speak, but her eyes return to mine, and her look makes me shut up. I think she knows what's on my mind, and she is not having it. She can be stubborn, but this time I have to be just as strong.

"I will get you out of here."

It takes me a second to realize what she is saying.

"What? No... you... must leave me here and... run... For our son. Please..."

My voice is barely a whisper, and she doesn't reply, just continues her mission to free my hands from the chains.

"Please..."

I'm pleading with her. I want her to be safe and far away from here. Her face is next to mine as she answers, too busy to look up:

"I'm not going anywhere without you. Don't even try to convince me."

I let out a small sigh, and the coughing starts again. She stops for a second, obviously alarmed.

"Please, I just want you to be safe."

I manage to whisper as the pain eases a bit. She looks at me and this time I realize the tears that cover her face.

"How could I live without you? And our son? Do you think he could live without his father? So please do me a favor and save your energy for the way out, instead of wasting it on trying to convince me."

She can hardly finish the sentence through her sobs, but I do understand it. All this time the only thing I thought about was to get her out of here, to get her into safety, no matter what. But the actual thought of losing her has always been unbearable. I know that I wouldn't be able to live without her, even if I got out of here alive. But the thought didn't cross my mind that she might feel the same. Somehow I thought that our son will compensate her for the loss. Judging from her expression, I was wrong.

This fills me with pride and joy, as I realize that she can't live without me either, but makes me feel sad, too, as I know I have very little chance of surviving this battle. A triumphant smile appears on her lips and she asks me if I can move my arms. I nod weakly, trying to hide the agony even the slightest movement is causing me. But with her, nothing goes unnoticed.

She helps me stay on my feet, and when she thinks I am stable enough, she moves on to her next target. I watch intently as her tiny hands grab the chains, pulling at them ever so gently, afraid to hurt me, looking for a way to take them off. I think I fall in love with her a little more that moment..

<u>**Other Books by Timea Tokes:**</u>

<u>**Paranormal Romance:**</u>
Her First Secret
Her Secret Admirer
His Secret Love
Their Last Secret
Her First And Last Secret Admirer

<u>**Erotic Short Stories:**</u>

<u>**BDSM:**</u>
A Special Cup of Coffee – Pain and Pleasure

<u>**Hotwife:**</u>
Stuck & Shared

<u>**Holiday Erotica:**</u>
Mistletoe Boss
Dating The Author (Why Choose)
My Hitch-Hiking Valentine
The Bucket List
The Bucket List 2 - Damsel in Distress
Truth or Dare?

<u>**Exhibitionist & Voyeur:**</u>
Squirm Under My Watch
How About the Rooftop?
Don't Make A Sound

<u>Paranormal Erotica:</u>
Conjured Lover

<u>The Plumber Series:</u>
Seducing the Plumber 1: Sweet Time Waiting
Seducing the Plumber 2: Sweet Torture

<u>The Escort Series:</u>
The Escort's Taxi Ride
The Escort's Taxi Ride 2
The Escort's Taxi Ride 3

<u>The Good Neighbor Series (Bisexual, Why Choose):</u>
The Good Neighbor – An Unexpected Threesome
The Good Neighbor – Tied up by the Knight
The Good Neighbor – In the Backseat
The Good Neighbor – The Massage
The Good Neighbor – Guilty Pleasures

<u>Sweet yet Naughty:</u>
Forgotten
Blue Highlights

<u>Gay:</u>
The Stranger

<u>Collections of Short Stories:</u>
You Had Me At Kinky
You Had Me At Steamy
You Had Me At Rough

Coming Soon:

The Plumber's Excuse (2020)
Kiss & Tell Tail 2 (2020)
A Cupid Mistake (2021)
Hell's Bride (2021)

Follow Timea Tokes on:

Amazon @timea_tokes

Twitter @timea_tokes

Facebook @herfirstsecret

Goodreads @timea_tokes

Sign up to her newsletter, and have a look at her blog for more bite-size erotica, paranormal romance, reviews and more:

www.timeatokes.com

<u>Note from the Author, Timea Tokes:</u>

~o~

My dear, lovely Reader, thank you for taking the time to read my story! I really hope you enjoyed it as much as I did writing it. As always, your feedback is highly valued and much appreciated.

Please do take the time to scroll to the end of the book and leave a review. It would mean the World to me!

And remember, this story is all about your pleasure.

On the next page, you can learn a bit more about me and why I write, but you will also find author interviews (and much more) on my website.

~o~

ABOUT THE AUTHOR

~o~

have been writing short stories and poems since a young age, but my ultimate goal was creating a novel. Or a series, rather. Now, with my four para rmal romance novels published, as well as more than 30 erotica titles under my belt, , I think I can say that it came true - but this only fuels my desire to write more. After all, we are allowed to dream the same dream (over and over again) - and that's exactly what I'm planning to do :)

I enjoy helping people in any way possible, and I really hope that my books will prove to be inspirational in a way. Whether readers are looking for a swift (and steamy) erotic story, or a paranormal romance, I want them to associate themselves with my characters and realize stuff about themselves in the process.

Yes, even the bad things. Because, in life, there is no black and white, only colors. Therefore, I don't think any of my characters are either good or bad, but rather a little bit of both.

Aren't we all?

Well, if you never had guilty thoughts, never had any self-confidence issues, or if you never wanted something (or someone) who belonged to someone else, then probably my books won't be for you. But, who knows, I might be able to show you a different perspective. I like to experiment with different genres, and new concepts and ideas.

I really enjoy learning as much as I can about people, what makes them tick (and live, laugh, cry, and sigh). In fact, I think our World (and those beyond) are so diverse, ten thousand lifetimes wouldn't be enough to explore it all. But one thing I truly believe in: those who belong in your life will find a way there. Therefore my stories are usually based on chance encounters and ordinary events that take an unexpected turn.

Like a blind date on Valentine's day, or a haircut, or a new job. Who says you can't meet someone 'accidentally'; while going to the hairdresser, someone you lost contact with 500 years ago? Trust me, you can. You just need to brace every day (and every book) with open eyes - and an open heart.

Just remember: my stories are all about you, and you alone. If they capture your attention (and your heart), then I've done my 'job'. I regularly try to release new content, both on Amazon and my blog. Please feel free to have a look, and sign up to my newsletter.

And, just so you know: I care about your opinion, very much so. Whether you liked my work or you didn't, I would be honored if you let me know what it meant for you. It would mean the world to me!

~o~

1. When did you create your first erotica story, and what was it about?

Well, my first story wasn't fully erotica, more a romance story. In fact, I never thought that one day I would write anything steamy. Not at all. I was shy, and grew up in an environment, where everything was taboo. Sharing my views on sex with anyone, let alone write about it? No way...

And yet, I soon had to realize that writing romantic stories couldn't happen without the couple getting it on eventually. Especially because the first four books series I created was about the same characters, and they are 100 pages each (which is a lot to go without including a sex scene every now and again). I must admit, I delayed the inevitable for as long as I could, just to realize later how much I enjoyed writing about sex.

Although my first attempts were very timid indeed, I tried to avoid being too explicit or descriptive. I concentrated on the romantic and paranormal aspect of it (the main characters dream about each other, and somehow when I was writing about the dreams, they gave me courage to be a bit braver).

But it wasn't until I started writing my erotic short stories in 2015, when I started to experiment. Well, if you have a look at 'The Good Neighbour', you can see how my explicitness and mood changed throughout the series.

I think I can say that this was the very first fully erotic story I created, fulfilling one of my secret fantasies (no, I don't have a hot neighbour, or at least I don't think I have, but the idea always fascinated me).

2. What (or who) inspired you to start writing erotica?

My own lack of courage, if I'm honest. All my friends were so open about their relationships and their fantasies, so I thought:

"Why do I have to be this way, when I want to explore everything that's out there?"

And as I have always enjoyed writing, I decided to try it out on paper. It started as a therapy I prescribed for myself, and then it escalated, taking me to places I never thought I would visit. I must say that I'm really glad I gave in to temptation.

3. What do you find most challenging when writing these stories?

To let them go when I finish writing them. I believe that it isn't possible, especially when I create a longer story. The characters, the feelings stay with me long after, as they become part of me for at least a little while.

Another aspect of it is that I keep thinking about what others read into them, and whether they convey their meaning in a way that I intended them to. But, just like when you give birth to a child, when writing a story as well you need to give it space after some time.

I once read a quotation (not sure where, or who said it, but it made me smile and I could definitely relate):

"I met the man of my dreams last night.. in chapter five…" *Sigh*

4. Do you write in other genres, and if yes, then would you consider mixing them with erotica?

Yes, and not sure. I ghost-write for a living, as well as create my own stories, which include romance, horror, thriller, fantasy, crime and more, but I'm not sure it would feel right to mix them with erotica. Mind that, I have had some strange requests that were a mixture, like fetish-horror, but it didn't actually include erotica. I suppose it could have, as it was about a foot fetish, which seems to be quite popular. Oh well, another thing to look at in the future :)

My favourite ones are psychological thrillers though, so I could probably turn one of those into erotica, but at the moment I'm thinking of a transition, rather than a mix. So, for example it would start as a thriller, but have a sexual ending. Hmm…

5. Have you written any stories that were inspired by real life events?

Yes. In fact, my very first story, 'Her First and Last Secret Admirer' (the four books I mentioned earlier) started with an actual recurring medieval dream, which I then implemented into the plot, creating a story and background for it. If it wasn't for that urge to put the whole thing into writing, I probably would never have picked up the courage to write at all. Now it is both in print and on Kindle, so I guess it was a nice bargain :)

I think that writing about real events, twisting them a little, but still keeping them close to your heart is an important process.

Also, that way you can relive those events over and over again, and others will keep guessing what was the real part in it.

Strangely enough, it adds to its mystery (and excitement, of course)...

6. What is your speciality and why?

I would say it's mixing the past with the present. I'm not an expert, but I also love to keep up the suspense until the end. Although this doesn't always come through in my erotic stories, as they are linear, but in my paranormal romance books, I draw a parallel between what happened 500 years ago and what's happening right now. It's difficult to explain without revealing the plot itself, but I do love to play with the mind of the reader, if you know what I mean.

7. Are there any topics you don't like writing about?

Now? Not really. If you asked me a few years ago, I would have said everything that involves sex ;)

I guess I just realized that I shouldn't say no, just because I don't know how something feels. If I don't try it, I will never know... If I'm not familiar with a topic, then I do my research, but not too many things scare me nowadays (without wanting to sound weird or vain).

8. Do you have any tips / warnings for newbie erotica writers?

Follow your dreams. You will get some ugly feedback (or none at all), but that doesn't mean that your work isn't appreciated. Don't take them personally, but accept them, so that they can serve as stepping stones, helping you improve your writing. We all make mistakes; that's what makes us human.

Personally, I couldn't wait to grab a physical copy of my books, and that made up for whatever negativity I got (but luckily it has only been minor stuff so far).

So, if you are thinking about writing, or if you already have a story or two, try to make them into a book, no matter how tiny it is. Trust me, as soon as you have it on your shelf, you will become a different person.

9. What is your favourite season and why?

Spring, because that's when everything comes to life. I just love to watch the flowers blossom and the world wake up from its winter slumber. I always feel like I'm reborn myself every time springs comes (I know, I'm a hopeless romantic).

www.ingramcontent.com/pod-product-compliance
Lightning Source LLC
Chambersburg PA
CBHW031003180726
47993CB00018B/1546